This book belongs to

_____

Written by Moira Butterfield
Illustrated by Rosalind Beardshaw
Designed by Lisa Sturley

This edition published by Parragon Books Ltd in 2014

Parragon Books Ltd
Chartist House
15–17 Trim Street
Bath BA1 1HA, UK
www.parragon.com

ISBN 978-1-4723-7720-3

Printed in China

Smile baby smile

PaRragon

Bath · New York · Cologne · Melbourne · Delhi
Hong Kong · Shenzhen · Singapore · Amsterdam

The sun shone.
The birds flew.
The flowers grew.

But the baby...

The sister tried singing.

The brother tried swinging.

The mummy said, **"Coo."**

The daddy said, "Boo!"

The sister played some pit-a-pat.

The brother wore a funny hat.

The mummy made
a shiny star.

The daddy drove around in the car.

But the baby...

The sister kissed
the baby's toes.

The brother kissed
the baby's nose.

The mummy hugged the baby tight.

The daddy kissed them
all goodnight.

Then the baby did a funny **burp**...

burp

...and then the baby...

The End